PRAISE FOR CIVIL BLOOD
BEST LEFT IN THE SHADOWS BOOK 2

"[A] lightning quick story of criminal confrontations, old feelings, and rousing fights... Gelineau and King have so much more to reveal before this mesmerizing tale is done."

– Bookwraiths

"The chemistry between these two was spectacular."

– Twin Reads

"It's gripping stuff, and as Gelineau and King gain confidence and experience, it's turning into a hell of a ride."

– One More

PRAISE FOR BEST LEFT IN THE SHADOWS

"Like with the previous *Ascended* books, I really love the characters and their dynamic. The female lead Alys is different from the heroines in *Reaper* and *Rend the Dark*, but she's just as complex and strong."

– White Sky Project

"The story was filled with gritty characters and dirty back streets, lies and deception. There was also this great sexual tension between Alys and Daxton that created a witty banter, which was so much fun to read."

– Paein and Ms4Tune

Praise for Faith and Moonlight
Part 1

"*Faith and Moonlight* is reminiscent of Terry Pratchett in that laced through the heavy atmosphere, array of emotion, and implausible magic is hope. That spirit of what might be lightens the feel considerablely, making for a delightful story."

– Rabid Readers Reviews

"Amazing, well-developed, and relatable characters combines with snappy, realistic dialogue and simple prose to make this coming of age story... a true fantasy gem."

– Cover2Cover

"A heartbreaking narrative that was so realistic at times, I forgot I was reading fantasy."

– Mama Reads, Hazel Sleeps

"You can really feel Roan's desire and dream to be something more and you can also feel Kay's frustration and struggle. And underneath all that you can practically touch how much they care about each other."

– White Sky Project

MARK GELINEAU
JOE KING

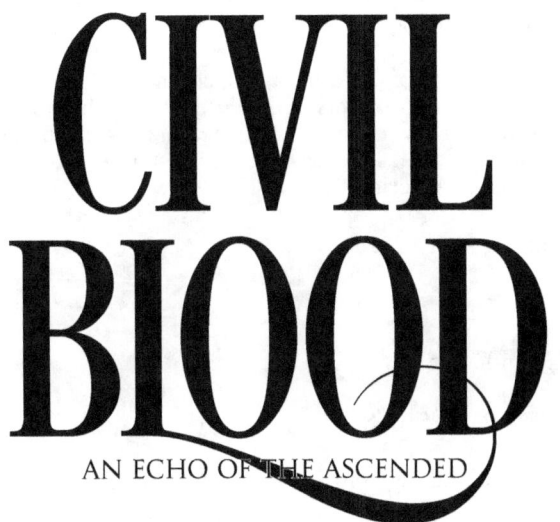

CIVIL
BLOOD

AN ECHO OF THE ASCENDED

First Printing: April 2016

v1.1

Gelineau and King

ISBN 978-1-944015-13-8

www.gelineauandking.com

ACT 1
SMOKE GETS IN YOUR EYES

The thing about a Lowside fire is that it smells different.

Different than any campfire you might have huddled around. Different than the occasional fires that sprang up in the more respectable parts of the capital. No, a fire in Lowside had a distinctive smell all its own.

People said it was because the buildings were older, but Alys knew better. She knew the strange undercurrent of nauseating sweetness that always carried on the wind came from the smell of burning flesh.

Because a Lowside fire always meant corpses.

She walked down the Street of Brewers, the familiar weight of Aunty on her back, the huge scythe swaying in time with her step. The smoke was thick in the air, that horrid sweetness cloying on her tongue. Her mood worsened with each ringing step of her bootheels on the cobblestones.

That bastard Keyburn.

She and Keyburn had been good for a lot of days and she enjoyed drinking at his place, the Olde Sportsman's Hall, on the odd night, but he was drawing on a lot of credit rousting her like this. It seemed like he'd sent every urchin and beggar in Lowside looking for her.

That meant he was desperate. And she was in no mood for desperate.

Alys turned onto Little Blood. The street name seemed maddeningly appropriate as the dying flames of the burning building ahead stained the night sky a ruddy crimson. It was ugly and unpleasant. Alys couldn't shake the feeling it was setting a deliberate tone for what was to come.

In the distance, she saw fire had spread between a number of cramped buildings. It was a lot of damage done fast. Cinderman's fire crews must have been drunk tonight to let the blaze go like it had.

Keyburn was in front of a building. His arms were crossed over his chest, but as he saw Alys approach, they fell to his sides. The movement was slight and natural, but it immediately set her on edge. Key kept his hands free and his arms loose, like he was expecting trouble.

Or like he intended it.

Alys grimaced. Shit. She and Keyburn went back a ways. She was going to be pissed if he made her kill him tonight.

"Ta, Alys," Keyburn said, raising his chin in greeting.

Alys ignored the pleasantry. "You been spreading my name from the Prionside Docks to the Night Circus, Key. You wanted me here, I'm here. Now, you want to tell me why?"

Alys had already noticed the two large bruisers by the entrance of the burned-out building. They made no attempt at subterfuge. In fact, they seemed to be doing their best to be noticeably menacing. It was kind of adorable, Alys thought.

Even as she dismissed their threatening posturing, her mind tried to piece together what the hell this was about. At first, she thought Keyburn might actually be stupid enough to make a play. It wasn't like him, but everything had that sort of feel to it.

"Something here needs your attention, Alys," Keyburn said, his voice tight.

Alys put her hands on her hips and leaned on her back leg. "Not interested," she said. "My trade is information and secrets, Key. Fires are the Cinderman's revenue stream. You're better off waiting on one of his fire crews."

"They're already here," he said before pointing toward the inside of the building.

"None of this looks like it's worth any of my business. Still not interested, Key."

"Trust me, Alys. You're going to want to see this."

Alys let out an exasperated sigh, but she followed him into the building.

Against the soot-stained brick wall, four bodies had been strung up by their hands, blood pooled beneath them on the wrecked floor. Someone had done them with a knife, that much was abundantly clear. Did them long and slow. With a skilled hand.

Keyburn spoke from beside her. "These men were one of the Cinderman's fire crews."

"So somebody didn't want to pay up proper to put the fire out and left the Cinderman a little message." Alys shrugged her shoulders. "Still not interested."

There was a wracking cough behind Alys. Standing there was Magda, Keyburn's bartender at the Sportsman's. Her clothes were ragged and her face was stained black with soot. Her usual yellow curls were lank and filthy. She coughed again.

"Magda lived in the building over there," Keyburn said. "When the fire sprung up, she scampered right and fast, but then she came across this little bit of theater here," he whispered. "It's alright, Magda. Tell her who did this. Tell her who you saw."

One red eye stared out from the bristles of hair as Magda pointed at Alys.

"You did it. You did the cutting on all of them." She gasped and wheezed, but managed to force the last words out before more coughing. "I saw it. It was you, Alys."

Alys looked from Keyburn to Magda then back to Keyburn's serious face. "Alright, Key. You got me," she said. "Now, I'm interested."

ACT 2
HEAVY IS THE HEAD THAT WEARS THE CROWN

Everything was just so damn shiny.

That was the problem, Dax realized. Everything in the palace seemed to gleam with a flawless, polished reflection. Light from the morning sun streamed through high windows, making every surface dance and sparkle.

It was all giving him one bastard of a headache.

A group of soldiers moved past him, marching in perfect harmony. The lead officer saluted crisply and Dax wondered if the man genuinely recognized him or if that was his reaction any time he saw someone in the northern wing.

Dax sighed heavily. There was a time when he had loved everything about the palace. Growing up in these halls, watching the soldiers in their finery, the palace staff, the nobles. Everything seemed magical. The beauty, the rich history resonating from every sculpture, painting, and tapestry captivated him.

When did it all start to feel so burdensome? So hollow? So false?

Oh, right.

Alys.

The stone steps underfoot were familiar from the years when his father had held the post of First Shield, captain of the palace guard. Now, Dax's brother, Marek, held the post, and their father served at the right hand of the king. They lived lives that Dax could not imagine.

And that he wanted no part of.

Two guards were stationed outside the office of the palace guard captain. Unlike the city guardsmen under Dax's command as justicar, these two wore shining gold breastplates instead of silver. They did not look at Dax and yet, as he approached, they both snapped to rigid attention.

Dax had a sudden urge to rap on their bright breastplates instead of knocking on the door, but promptly dismissed the idea. Alys was a bad influence on him, he thought ruefully.

"Come," said a familiar voice from inside.

Dax opened the heavy wooden door and smiled at his brother behind the large desk.

"It's nice to see you still know your way around the old place," Marek said, standing and coming over to embrace him. He was taller than Dax, his hair lighter, but they shared the same eyes. They'd both inherited them from their father.

Dax grinned. "Fortunately, they haven't changed a thing in these halls since I was six and you broke that statue of Aedan and Talan."

Sputtering, Marek shook his head. "I broke it? If you remember correctly, little brother, it was your wild swinging that broke it. And I took the heat from Father for it."

"Yes," Dax shot back. "Because you suspended me by my britches from the tip of Aedan's sword and left me dangling like a fish on a hook!"

Marek paused, and then broke out in a loud laugh. "By the First Ascended, I'd forgotten that. That was hilarious!"

"And you wonder why I rarely come to visit, brother."

Stepping back, Marek gave him an appraising look. "You needn't have dressed in such finery for me, Daxton."

Dax looked down at his clothes. He had dismissed the usual Highside finery soon after his posting in Lowside, and the long, gray magistrate coat he still wore now looked worn and ragged. It hadn't occurred to him to change.

Dax shrugged. "No sense looking like a mark. I'll let the sharp hands have a go at your bits of shine over mine, Marek."

Marek shook his head and gave Dax a small smile. "Now you're even starting to sound like her, Dax."

Immediately, Dax's jovial mood soured. "Alys is not—"

Marek put up his hands in a gesture of supplication. "Easy, Dax. I liked her. I still do, for that matter. I have nothing against Alys." He caught Dax's eye. "It is you that I worry about, brother. I remember the last time all too well. It was not easy for me to watch you go through that. I would not wish to see my brother in such pain ever again."

Dax nodded slowly. "There is a lot from that time that I regret, but I am a better man for coming through that crucible, Marek. I am in Lowside for justice. Not for Alys. I know where the lines are now."

Marek stared at him for a bit and then nodded. "I am glad to hear that, little brother." His lips turned up at the corners and Dax recognized the same mischievous smile that meant trouble when they were boys. "Because I don't think I could take any more nights of you crying alone in your room." He started laughing. Dax stared daggers at him, but Marek ignored it. "The chief steward had the entire kitchen crew searching for a bat's nest in the walls, because he refused to believe that such wailing and squealing could come from a human being."

Dax tried to retain his icy countenance, but the memory of the fastidious, old steward's hopeless search broke him and he joined his brother in laughing. That had been a long time ago, a lifetime really, and it felt good to laugh about it.

It felt like burying the past.

He laid his hand on his brother's shoulder. Though Dax did not miss the palace in the least, he did miss Marek. Marek was eight years older than Dax and had practically raised him while their father tended to the kingdom's important matters.

"It is good to see you again," Dax said.

"Likewise," Marek said, smiling warmly.

"So," Dax said, clapping his hands together, "what drove you to summon me so urgently? Is this a personal meeting or some matter of state?"

"A bit of both, actually," Marek said. "Come with me."

Dax followed his brother out of the office. As they walked, Marek talked casually. "I have to hand it to you, Dax. No one knows how to get under father's skin better than you do." He chuckled. "With your choice of any posting in Resa, you maneuver yourself into being a justicar of the Second District."

"Father did not figure into that decision at all," Dax replied. "I felt like that was where I could do the most good."

"Of course, but it didn't hurt that you knew it would make him furious."

Dax smiled. "Well, that wasn't exactly a negative, no."

Laughing, Marek nodded. "Of course, but just as you now have your new job, I too have my position," he said. Dax felt a slight change in Marik's mood come with a shift in tone and topic. "As First Shield, my charge is first and foremost to protect the royal family." He stopped and, as Dax halted as well, Marek fixed him with a serious look. "And fight it as you might, little brother, you are a part of that family."

"Marek—"

"I have my duty, Daxton. To my kingdom and to my family. And I will see that duty done."

Dax shook his head. "No one cares about the seventh in line to the throne, Marek," he said in exasperation.

Marek took a step closer and lowered his voice. "They do when they make their home in Lowside," he said.

Before Dax could reply, Marek turned and entered a double door. Reluctantly, Dax followed.

Inside the room, five palace guards, resplendent in golden breastplates, waited at perfect attention. Dax wondered how long they had been standing there.

As he and Marek entered, the first soldier, a young woman with short blonde hair and large eyes, took a step forward. "Presentation!" she said with a confident note of authority.

As one, each of the soldiers snapped a salute directed not at Marek, but Dax.

That immediately made him nervous.

Marek stepped over to the young woman in charge of detachment. "This is Sergeant Laurel," Marek said. "She is exceptional and an expert on Lowside. She assembled these men herself."

Raising an eyebrow, Dax looked from his brother to the young sergeant and back. "For what purpose?"

That seemed to catch Marek by surprise. "You, Dax. They are your new protection detail."

Dax couldn't help himself. He laughed loud and long at that. "You can't be serious, Marek."

"I am intensely serious, Dax. I told you I intend to see my duty done. You are my responsibility."

Dax's laughter faded. "I don't want any special treatment."

Rather than Marek, it was Sergeant Laurel who answered, "With respect, Lord Ellis, it is only treatment befitting your station." Her voice was clipped and formal, immediately getting on Dax's nerves.

"You mean my father's station. And with respect, Sergeant," he replied, repeating her words back, "your fine detail here wouldn't last a day in Lowside."

Laurel tilted her head slightly and clasped her hands behind her back. "I think you would be quite surprised, Lord Ellis. In Highside, we're shining soldiers. In Lowside, we can be whatever you need from us. But either way, we are yours."

Dax looked back to his brother. "No," he said.

Marek remained impassive. "You are in Lowside now, Dax. You put yourself there and you have to accept what that means. You have put yourself in the world of Pious Black, and there, in that dark world, you will need allies. You will need protection."

Dax's head was shaking before his brother finished. "You speak about Pious Black like he's one of the ancient Ruins, a monster stalking the streets of Lowside. He's a crime boss."

"He is *the* crime boss," Marek corrected. "And he is more Ruin than man. He's more blood on his hands than any of those ancient terrors ever spilled. And most of that blood is women and children. Know why? Because he kills the weakness out of his people, Dax, and makes them depend only on him. That's the world you're walking into. A world of monsters."

"Believe me, I know the kind of man he is. There's not a minute I'm in Lowside that I'm not looking over my shoulder for Pious Black. But if Pious killed me, it would be open war between Lowside and the Crown. He would never do something so foolish. It would be bad for business. It's in his best interest to keep me alive."

"You play a dangerous game," Sergeant Laurel said. "Pious Black is the most feared and wanted man in Aedaron. He nearly killed your father."

Dax's blood turned cold as memories of that terrible night clawed at the edge of his mind. His composure shaken, he rounded on the young woman, "It was the failure of the Royal Guard that led to that near tragedy," he said, staring hard at her. "If I were you, Sergeant, I would be more concerned with my father's continued safety than with mine." Dax looked back to his brother. "We are done here, Marek."

For a moment, Marek said nothing. Then, he gave a small nod and snapped his fingers. Immediately, Sergeant Laurel returned to attention and saluted. Marek returned it before leading Dax from the room.

The two were quiet as they walked to the front gates. The silence was heavy and tense. Dax could not help feeling like he had been lured into a trap.

Marek sighed. "I can see it on your face, Dax, but you have to understand where I am coming from. Stop and think for just a moment about that."

It took a lot, but Dax nodded. "I get it, but I don't need protection, Marek. And most assuredly not from them."

"They're good people, Dax. Brave. Loyal." Marek's face grew more serious and his voice lowered. "But if you are not going to take them, then at least listen to these words. Lowside is not just a slum, Dax. You know that. It feeds on itself. It's organized now and far more dangerous than even you can imagine. Pious Black is the hand that feeds it and he is growing it for some dark purpose." He dipped his chin, catching Dax's eyes and holding his focus. "And Alys is caught in that world. I'm not saying she is to blame, but her world is darker than you know."

Dax put a hand on his brother's shoulder. "I love you, Marek. You've always looked out for me and I will never forget that, but if what you say is true, about Lowside and the danger it poses, then isn't that all the more reason it needs someone to bring justice and light to that darkness?"

Marek looked at him for a long moment. "And you're sure it is Lowside you are so intent on saving?"

Smiling, Dax shrugged. "Believe me, big brother. Alys doesn't need saving. She doesn't need my help."

***

Back in Lowside, the air seemed colder. Dax couldn't help noticing the change as he walked into the Second District Precinct House. He nodded to some of his men as he passed and entered his office.

Alys was seated behind his desk.

"Finally," she said in exasperation, springing to her feet.

"Alys? What?"

She walked past him and grabbed his hand. "Come on," she said. "I need your help."

ACT 3
KNOCKING THE DUST OFF

To the casual eye, the small shop was a mass of clutter with strange curios and eclectic assortments crowding every shelf and table.

But Alys's eye was anything but casual.

Though she had not been in the shop for years, she still recognized every object. Each was in its proper place, just as it had been the last time she had walked through that door. She called it a shop, but she could not remember anyone ever purchasing anything. In all likelihood, the old bastard who ran it wouldn't sell anyway. That would mean change and that just couldn't be. Nothing ever changed in the old man's shop. That was the way he liked it.

"Don't touch anything," she whispered.

From the corner of her eye, she saw Dax pull his hands back from a strangely shaped skull resting on a cramped shelf beside the door. "Wouldn't dream of it," he said.

She had to hand it to him. When she explained that someone was blackening her name around Lowside, he hadn't asked questions. When she told him she needed him to come along, he had come. No hesitation. Dax never lacked for loyalty. If anything, he had an overabundance of it.

"Not buying or selling right now," said a voice before a ruddy, round face peeked out from behind a towering pile of old books on the other side of the room. Red hair, thinning on top and fading to white on the bottom, was slicked back from the big head while heavy jowls pulled down in a perpetual frown. The man's eyes squinted and tracked from Alys to Dax and back. "But you already know that, don't you, girl?"

"I do, old man. Just like I also know you've been hearing my name spoke a lot in the last two nights."

"Not so old that I don't hear the street whispers. And they're practically screaming your name lately."

Alys stepped deeper into the room. "My name perhaps, but not my hand. Someone's pinning it to me, bright and shiny as you please."

A guttural laugh came from the old man. "Imagine that. You getting the squeeze for someone else's sins."

"The irony is not lost on me, old man."

The laughter stopped. "Then perhaps you tell me why you've come gracing my fine establishment."

"You know people," Alys said simply.

"I know lots of people."

It had been enough years that Alys forgot how big a pain in her ass the old man could be. "I need to see the Cinderman. Clear things up."

"I'd say you do," he replied. "Someone's out there. Sharp-edged and moonlight quick, way I hear it. They lit up the Cinderman's crew and made sure there were witnesses to pin the penny for it on you, girl."

"Wasn't me," Alys said simply.

"Course it wasn't," the old man replied before slowly shaking his head. "But doesn't matter. The Cinderman has no time for you now, girl. He's pulled back to the Foundry. The thought of you alone has him pissing himself so much he's likely to put those fires out all by himself now."

Alys smiled her most charming smile. "That's where you come in. I need muscle," she said, cutting to it. "A lot of muscle. And quick."

The old man laughed again, the sound echoing in the small shop. "Only you, Alys. Only you would seek to assuage a man's fear of you by raising a small army and assaulting him."

Dax, having been surprisingly quiet throughout the exchange, stepped up and whispered in her ear, "Muscle? Assaulting? What exactly do you have planned?"

She sighed. He had been doing so well without the questions. "Relax, Justicar," she said with a smile. "It's for show. Everything's for show in Lowside."

"Like showing up at Cinderman's door with a mob of rough-and-readys. Or even a king's justicar at your side." the old man said with a wink.

Dax scowled, but Alys continued, "The biggest fights are won before they're fought. Especially down here. We need to show equal force or the Cinderman will never negotiate a meeting." She waited for Dax to give a small nod then looked back to the counter. "So are you in, old man, or should I let you go back to collecting dust?"

The man opened one eye before shrugging. "What the hell. Been a long time since I was out amongst the shade folk. Could use a bit of excitement." He dismounted from his stool and stretched his long arms out, pulling his shirt's fabric tight across his ample belly before walking to Dax and extending a hand. "Name's Donner," he said.

"Dax," Dax replied, taking the hand.

"You prefer the short version, then? I think it suits you better than 'Your Lordship.'"

Dax smirked. "I always thought so."

Alys turned and walked out of the store. As she did, she heard them talking.

"Just like old times?" Dax asked.

"Ha!" Donner said. "For your sake, let's hope not!"

Alys tensed slightly.

"What do you mean?" Dax asked.

As they exited the shop, Donner flipped a little, wooden sign hanging from a nail by the door to proclaim the shop closed. "Last time Alys had a crew together is when we almost killed your father," Donner said with a grin.

ACT 4
TWO FOR FLINCHING

"That's treason," Dax said as they waited in an alleyway.

He saw Alys blow a black strand of hair out of her eyes in exasperation. Donner had left them about a half hour before, off on his mission to recruit what Alys called muscle. The entire time the man had been gone, Dax kept recalling his words. That night's memories circled in his mind until finally he had to give them voice.

Alys responded in typical fashion. "Keep your voice down," she whispered.

"Treason," he repeated.

She turned toward him. "Technically, killing your uncle, the king, would be treason. In Lowside, talk of killing your father is practically dinnertime conversation."

His frown deepened. "This is a serious matter, Alys."

"You're damned right it's serious. That night got a lot of good people killed and it burned more bridges for me than you know."

"With who?" Dax snapped. "With Pious Black? The one who turned you against me?"

Alys gave a bitter laugh. "You don't know a damned thing about Pious."

"I know he is the only one that could ever shape your choices."

She gave him a long, hard look. "No," she said simply. "He wasn't the only one." Dax felt her dark gaze pierce his soul. "But he was the only one that I trusted that hasn't ever let me down."

Before Dax could respond, Donner appeared around the corner.

"You got them?" Alys asked.

Donner nodded. "Brickhouse Boys. None too bright, but they're honest in the way that only the truly simple can be. That bag of coins you provided bought them nicely. They're on their way to the Foundry."

Alys gave a curt nod before marching down the alley, leaving Dax and Donner behind.

Donner looked to Dax. "You went and said something stupid, didn't you, boy?"

Dax bristled at the term. "I was just wondering if her old friend Pious Black still had her ear."

"Dangerous thoughts," he said in a low voice. "What's your curiosity with Pious Black?"

"Pious Black rules Lowside, doesn't he? I am a justicar for the Second District. That makes him my business."

"Pious Black doesn't run Lowside, boy. He is Lowside." Donner blew out a long breath and the tension on his face eased slightly. "You don't know what Lowside was like before Pious. The streets ran with blood. It was a hellish place. Pious brought order to that chaos."

Dax stared at the rickety, old buildings towering over the alley. Old wood was exposed everywhere, like ribs on a starving man. In the distance, he heard a man crying in pain. "It doesn't seem all that different now to me." From behind, Dax heard Donner sigh.

"It wouldn't to you, Lord Ellis," the old man said. "In Highside, order and control come from edicts and proclamations. Here, it comes from putting a blade in the back of the right man at the right moment."

At that moment, Dax went cold. He realized he had been so caught up in the argument with Alys that he had dropped his guard. That was something he could not afford in Lowside. Donner had been there when a group of Pious Black's murderers came for Dax's father. Donner knew Pious Black. Old man or not, that made him dangerous.

Dax turned, putting his back toward the alley's wall. "We'd best catch up to Alys," he muttered, motioning for Donner to proceed him from the alleyway.

The old man looked at the gesture and smiled broadly. He walked past Dax before nodding. "Keeping me ahead of you and not at your back now? Seems Alys has taught you a thing or two after all. Perhaps there's hope for you yet." Laughing, he led them into the street.

***

Their destination loomed large, dominating the dirty, gray skyline of Lowside and contributing its own darkness as its tall chimneys spewed black smoke. This was the place Alys described as the Cinderman's center of power. The Foundry.

The Cinderman ran the fire brigades in Lowside, but unlike the guardsmen who dealt with fires in the rest of the captial, the rules here were different. Here, if a home or business caught fire, the Cinderman's crews would be there, quick as you please, if you had the coin to pay their price.

This was one of many practices Dax was looking forward to ending now that he was a justicar for Lowside.

As they closed in on the building, rough-looking men began to join them. When each group fell into place, they gave Donner a small nod. One or two even looked familiar. Dax realized they likely had been held in his precinct house for one crime or another.

Muscle, Alys had said. It appeared she had it now.

Alys joined the group about a block from the Foundry gates, stepping from shadows and slipping between men to walk beside Dax and Donner.

Dax leaned toward her as they walked. "This is your idea of a show of force to help negotiations?"

"Why?" she replied. "Don't they look forceful?"

"They look like a damned army, Alys!" Dax retorted.

Ahead, men and women poured from the Foundry, coming to the open gates to challenge the approaching group. Quite a few were armed. Tension was thick in the air.

"I think you are sending the wrong message," Dax added.

"Unclench, Dax. It's fine. Just tell them who you are and we can start to negotiate. Simple as pie."

Incredulous, Dax jerked to a halt. "Me? What?"

All around, the toughs Donner had assembled stopped, glaring and posturing at the Cinderman's forces arrayed before the Foundry. Dax had never seen a Lowside riot before and now it appeared he was liable to start one.

Alys rested a hand on his arm. "It's fine. You walk up with me. You hold up your badge of office so everyone knows the justicar is here. Then, I request an audience with the Cinderman."

"Hold that badge up high and proud there, boy. You are the law in Lowside," Donner said, clapping him on the back. "Well, the king's law, anyway."

Together, the three made their way through the crowd and approached the gate. As they did, a group of Cinderman's troops met them. The lead one had a web of old burn scars spanning the left side of his face, pulling his mouth into a perpetual, half-snarl. He stopped directly before them and crossed his arms.

Drawing himself taller, Dax raised his badge high for all to see. "I am Lord Daxton Ellis," he announced. "King's magistrate and justicar of the Second District. I am here to open negotiations between—"

And then Alys smashed her fist into the burned man's nose.

Immediately, the scene devolved into chaos. Both sides burst like water from a ruptured dam and Dax was washed away on the tide. Everywhere, fists and boots thudded flesh. Amidst the tumult, Dax could not discern friend from foe. That is, if he even had friends in this wild melee.

Damn it, Alys.

Alys and Donner were nowhere to be seen amongst the pandemonium.

A fist caught the side of Dax's head, spinning him around and knocking him backwards into someone. He scrambled to stay upright, grabbing a man's shirt for support. The surprised man drew back a fist. Dax lashed out, punching the man's mouth. He felt teeth break beneath bone and his hand stung with pain.

Another combatant bore down upon Dax, but before he could engage the man, a roar sounded high above as a gout of flame blasted from a tall chimney.

The fighting paused.

A voice called out from above, "Enough! Stand down. All is fine!"

On one of the upper balconies, Dax saw Alys. Beside her, his bald head gleaming from the flame, was the Cinderman. Even at this distance, he seemed resplendent in ornate robes lined with gold.

The Cinderman bellowed again, "There is no quarrel here. Alys has come for parley and I have welcomed her!" Then, he leaned over the railing and scanned the crowd. "And I would have our honorable guest, the justicar, brought forth in safety to join us."

Alys nodded and waved her fingers at Dax. At that signal, her hired thugs faded away from the melee. Dax stared at her for a moment longer before realizing he stood alone in front of the Cinderman's men.

He looked at a man directly across from him. "So, should I show myself up?" Dax asked. He tried to offer a genial smile, but the side of his pained, punched face was starting to swell. His hand ached and bled.

The man simply pointed toward the Foundry's main door and then walked inside. Dax followed nursing his hurt hand.

The moment he entered the large building, heat hit him. All around, streams of molten metal poured into dark iron casting bins, glowing bright white as it flowed.

Alys was all smiles as she waited for Dax at the top of a long staircase.

"I hope you gave as good as you got, Justicar," she said, pointing to his cheek.

"What the hell was that all about?" Dax snapped. "One minute I'm standing there and the next thing I know you start a damn riot."

"Technically, it was a brawl, or perhaps a gang fight; definitely not a riot, Dax."

Dax grimaced. "You know, you are nowhere near as cute or endearing as you think you are."

Alys shook her head dismissively. "We both know that's a lie, but that's not the point. Could've been a riot, but I knew the fact that you were there would keep it subdued."

"Subdued?" Dax spat.

"Definitely. Punches instead of knives when the law's about." For a moment, Alys's face seemed to soften. "Look, Dax, I had to get in to see the Cinderman face to face. Had to get my blade to his throat."

Dax stared back in confusion before raising his eyes. "To show him if you wanted him dead, he would be dead right now."

Now, Alys smiled fully. "You're starting to think like a Lowsider, Dax. Yes, exactly. Now he knows it wasn't me."

"You could have told me, you know?" Dax said. "I would still have gone forward with it."

"Yes, and if it had gone south and there had been blood in the streets, what would you have said to your superiors? 'She promised me it would be fine'? No. This way, whatever happened, I, the dark-hearted devil of Lowside, was responsible for seducing you into my wicked scheme."

"So you did it to protect me?" Reaching up to feel his swollen face, Dax frowned. "I am so grateful," he mumbled.

"Admit it," she said. "This way was way more fun."

She gestured behind her to a set of broken doors. "Come on. Donner should have old Cin calmed down enough for a conversation now."

Inside, the large room was as lavishly appointed as any Highside mansion, only there was no taste or decorum shown in the furnishings. Every accoutrement seemed chosen based on ostentation rather than practicality; shining gold and dark velvet were very much the order of the day.

In the center of it all sat the Cinderman. Now that Dax had a closer look, he was not nearly so impressive. The bald head showed rough stubble where he had not recently shaved and the fine robes that appeared so grand on the balcony now seemed stained and ill fitting. But, more than anything else, it was the manic cast to his bulging eyes that drew Dax's attention. Those terrified eyes went directly to Alys when she entered.

"You gave your word, Alys. Gave your word!" he spat through wine-stained lips.

"Like I just told you, Cin. I have no quarrel with you. We have a common enemy in this. Someone is using my name to come at you."

"Not just the name. Not just the name, Alys." The Cinderman began to pace. "I questioned witnesses myself. And the few from each crew left alive. She looked like you. Fought like you."

Alys frowned. "You know it wasn't me," she said, her voice cold. "I wouldn't have left anyone to come back to you, if it had been me."

The Cinderman froze and gave her a hard look. For a moment, Dax saw the man who had carved himself a captaincy under the reign of Pious Black, regaining his reputation as one of the most feared men in Lowside. It crumbled as his face fell. "I lost it, Alys," he whispered, despair overtaking him.

Crossing her arms over her chest, Alys shrugged. "Lost what?" she asked, her voice sounding almost bored.

Eyes wide, the Cinderman took two darting steps toward her. "It!" he hissed, punctuating the syllable with the weight of his entire world.

As the sound faded, Dax saw something he had never seen before. Alys looked shocked.

Shocked and, maybe, afraid.

"Shit," she said.

Then, she was up from the table and heading toward the door at the other end of the room. "Your business is your business, Cin. I want no part of this."

"You're already a part of it, Alys! Whoever this is made you a part of it."

Alys stopped in her tracks. "Shit!"

Dax eased over to Donner. "What are they talking about?" he whispered to the old man. "Do you know?"

Donner rubbed the back of his hand across his chin. "It's a Lowside bedtime story. Mothers tell their children of the secret treasures of Pious Black, held by each of his trusted captains. Up-and-coming cutters and window-men dream of pulling a score and filching them, instantly making a name for themselves."

Dax listened intently before looking at the despondent Cinderman. Clearly, this was no mere story. "What was it then?"

Alys cut them off. "What it is isn't important," she said, her voice hard. She walked back to the table and practically collapsed into a chair. "What the hell happened, Cin?"

The Cinderman shook his head. "I started hearing things. Just vague rumors, but enough to let me know. Someone knew about it. Knew what I had and they were coming for it, so I moved it. Wanted to get it somewhere safer."

Alys stared at him incredulously before shaking her head. "You damn fool. You flinched. She baited you and you flinched. You put it right into her hands."

Cinderman walked to where Alys sat and crouched before her, almost kneeling. "She knew, Alys. She knew where my crew was. Hit them. Took it. I thought it had to be you. No one else would know about it. Only the captains and your old crew."

Dax saw her tense. The muscles in her neck stood out like whipcords. She slowly turned and looked to Donner. Next to Dax, the old man had gone perfectly still. Then, almost too small to notice, he shook his head.

"Can't be," Donner said. "She's dead."

Alys closed her eyes. "No body, old man. No body, no death. And she could pull it off. Knew me well enough to present herself as me. Even to those with a keen eye."

Donner shifted his head side to side. "She always had a knack for mimicry," he agreed.

Alys opened her eyes and leaned back in her chair. "It seems the Briarthorn is alive and well. And she's sending me one hell of a message." With that, Alys stood.

The Cinderman looked up at her. "What about me, Alys?"

"What about you, Cin?" Alys said without looking down. "She came at you. You flinched. You're done. If the Briarthorn doesn't get you, Pious surely and purely will." She stepped over the horrified former captain and walked to where Dax and Donner stood.

"And what will you be doing now, girl?" Donner asked, his voice low and serious.

Dax saw her jaw tighten before she gave a half-shrug. "I'm going to find the Briarthorn, old man. And I'm not going to flinch."

ACT 5
SINS OF THE PAST

The Olde Sportsman's Hall was typically quiet with still a few hours to go till sunset. The space around the rat pit was empty and the sawdust on the floor was free of blood. Alys sat at the bar, nursing a drink. Magda had taken Dax in the back to mend his face and hand.

The old man came in and took the stool next to Alys.

"You put the word out?" she asked him.

"Yep, it's done. Soon as Half-Penny Speaks comes crawling out from whatever hole he's hiding in, we'll know."

Alys nodded. "Looks like we wait then." She grabbed the bottle and slid it across the polished wood bartop.

After pouring himself a dram, the old man drained his drink and leaned on the bar. "When are you planning to cut the kid loose? He's in over his head."

"He'll be fine. He's been in over his head since he got to Lowside."

Donner chuckled. "I'd say for a fair bit before even then, Alys. Likely from the moment you walked into his life." He chuckled once more. "Poor bastard."

She raised an eyebrow. "What's this, old man? You warming up to him?"

"Hell no," he responded. "Don't think for a second I forgot what he's responsible for. Because of him, a lot of good blood got spilled. Hell, in a way, he's responsible for all this mess with the Briarthorn right now."

Eyes hard, Alys set her cup on the bar. "What happened that night isn't on him," she said, slowly and deliberately. "It's on me. I'm the one who made the decision."

The old man did not raise his voice, but he matched her intensity. "And it cost," Donner said. "You had a shot on the bastard. *The* bastard," he hissed with emphasis. "High Chancellor Ellis himself, may the rats eat his eyes." He stared for a minute and then sighed. "Whole wide world would have been a better place if that man hadn't been allowed to keep living in it."

Alys downed her drink without looking at him. "Like I said, it's on me."

"Yes, it is," Donner agreed. "Always will be. Especially while you're sharing time once again with his son." The old man shifted his considerable bulk around to face her. "Why'd you even bring him along? You didn't need him to meet old Cinderman and you certainly don't need him to track Briar." He fixed Alys with a look. "You're weaker when he's around."

"You worry too much, old man. I got me my own personal justicar and I'm sharper now than I've ever been."

Donner laughed. "I know you don't believe that little old lie," he said, "because I sure as hell don't believe it and you're twice as sharp as me and far less tolerant of bullshit."

"I should have left you in your shop," Alys said, shaking her head.

"But then you wouldn't be benefiting from my sage advice." He spun his glass on the wooden countertop. "Just tell me you're not trying to see if you can trust him again," he said quietly. "Highside toff like that, he'll be dead loyal to you ninety-nine out of a hundred times. But that hundredth time, girl, that time when you really need him, then he'll let you down." With a finger, he tipped his empty glass over, rattling it onto the bar. "Just like he did back then."

"Won't come to that, old man. I won't let it. I'm not that lovestruck little girl anymore," Alys said.

"No?"

Alys gave him a cold, hard grin. "Try me, old man."

ACT 6
PENNY FOR YOUR THOUGHTS

In the back of the Olde Sportsman's Hall, Dax sat at a rickety table while Magda carefully wrapped a bandage around his injured hand.

Now that the adrenaline had faded, Dax began to sort through what he had overheard. There was much he didn't know. That was charitable, if he was being totally honest. He had no idea what was going on.

Winding the coarse bandage, Magda spoke without raising her eyes, "Sounds like big happenings. Trying to figure it all out?"

Dax gave a small nod. "Something like that."

"My advice?" Magda asked. "Don't."

Surprised, Dax turned to look at her fully.

The bartender applied pressure and his bones ached as she tightened the wrapping. "The surest way to find trouble in Lowside is to go looking for it."

"Alys is already in trouble. I'm just here to help her out of this mess," Dax said.

Magda looked up and gave him a smile. "You're a sweetin and a charmer true, boy. I can see why our Alys is so soft on you." She tightened the dressing a final time and Dax made a small yelp. "Ever think it isn't your place to do so, though?"

Dax rubbed at his bandaged hand as she released it. "She asked me," he said.

Gathering her supplies, Magda looked at him. "Lowside is not streets and alleys," she said. "It's a twisted web of lies and deceptions, and its layers upon layers of it. So much so that it starts becoming difficult to tell if you're the spider or the fly."

"Is that your warning, Magda? You think I'm a fly?" Dax asked.

Magda paused before looking him in the eye and shaking her head. "No, what I'm trying to say is it doesn't matter which you are, because while the spiders and the flies are sorting themselves out, nobody notices the owls in the shadows getting ready to eat up both of them."

She picked up her wrappings and medicines. "Get out of Lowside while you can, Lord Ellis. You ain't never gonna see the owls. Not until it's too late."

***

Alys tossed Dax his long, gray coat when he walked back into the common room. "About time, Justicar Ellis. Time to get moving."

Dax rubbed at his head, already aching from the shot he had taken in the brawl. "Where is it we are off to?"

"To pick up her trail," Alys said. Then, she was out the door.

Dax said nothing as he followed Donner into the Lowside night.

If anything, the streets of Lowside were busier at night. That would take Dax some getting used to; the natural rhythms of day and night were too ingrained to be overwritten by a few short months working the streets of Lowside.

Quickening his steps, Dax caught up to Alys and walked aside. Donner ambled along on her other side. "You know how to find this Briarthorn?" Dax asked. "How'd you track her down?"

"Simple as bleeding," Alys said. "Clearly, she's back in the game, but she hasn't made herself known."

"Oh, she's been plenty public, girl. Just as you, that's all," Donner replied.

Alys nodded. "Exactly, and she's done a fair enough job to get even people who know me, like Magda, to bite. But she can't be me every minute, can she?"

"Which means she needs a place to hide," Donner finished.

Dax frowned. "But it's Lowside. Nothing here but places to hide."

"Very true," Alys said, "but combine that with what we've seen of her activities since she started back up. She hit Cinderman right and hard. Damn well dismantled him. That takes knowledge of his crews, his safe houses, his whole operation. Intimate knowledge."

Donner rubbed his chin while they walked. "So it has to be someone that knew Briar, but had some connection to the Cinderman."

"And, knowing Briar," Alys added, "she's going to have used someone I really don't like. And who doesn't like me."

Laughing, Donner shook his head. "Which brings us to Half-Penny Speaks."

Dax could barely keep up. "What's a 'half-penny speaks'?"

"Not a what. A who," Donner said. "Ran with Alys and the crew for a while. Proved himself to be a bit... unreliable when it came to keeping things quiet."

Dax turned the name over in his head. "Is that how he got the name? For a half-penny, he'll speak?" He laughed. "There really is an infatuation with creative naming conventions down here, isn't there?"

Donner's ruddy face was set and serious. "Names have meaning, boy. It is one of the few things that is true both Highside and Lowside. Isn't that right, Honorable Justicar Lord Daxton Ellis?"

Dax said nothing, but the old man's point was not lost.

Alys shot Dax a look before continuing. "After I cut him loose though, Half-Penny bounced around a bit, but he's been flush lately." Her mouth drew into a triumphant grin. "Because he's been working the fire crews. The Cinderman's fire crews."

Alys moved quickly and they followed through the twists and turns of Lowside streets before finally coming to a halt in front of a small flat at the base of a rundown tenement building. The place had one window, both steamed and stained, a door of banded metal and rotting wood. Though it had not rained for days, Dax heard a constant drip above their heads as they stood by the door.

"And this right here," she said, gesturing to the building behind her, "is where our geriatric gentleman," she said, gesturing to Donner, "has discovered Half-Penny Speaks makes his home."

Dax looked expectantly at Alys, waiting for her to climb the side of the building or break the window to gain entrance to Half-Penny Speaks's home.

Instead, she rapped her knuckles against the door.

There was scurrying inside before a small peephole opened in the door. A red-rimmed eye peered through and then grew wide.

"Oh no!" said a high-pitched voice behind the door.

"Oh yes," Alys responded, her teeth bared in a wolfish smile. "We will have words, Half-Penny. Best for you if you open the door smartish so we can begin."

There was the slightest pause, the barest moment where Dax wondered if the man was going to resist, before the sound of a heavy bolt being withdrawn came through. Then, a second. Finally, a third sounded before the door opened and Half-Penny Speaks ushered them in.

At first glance, Half-Penny Speaks resembled a human rat with red-tinted, sunken eyes and a small, thin mustache framing a mouth of unclean teeth. He had a stringy build and barely came up to Dax's shoulders. Half-Penny quickly shut the door after they entered. As he did, Dax saw his right hand was a mangled claw, the first two fingers missing.

Half-Penny gestured toward Dax's own bandaged hand. "What? You piss her off too?" he said in his high, reedy voice.

"I didn't take your fingers because you pissed me off, Half-Penny," Alys cut in, her voice hard. "I took them because your inability to keep your mouth shut almost ruined some very important evenings, once upon a time." She pulled out the only chair in the one-room hovel and sat, crossing her legs. "Fortunately for you, I now find I have need of your talent for sharing information."

Half-Penny grinned. "Sure, Alys. Anything I can do for an old friend. What is it you want to know?" he asked, but there was a manic nervous energy, practically panic, in his words.

"I want to know where the Briarthorn is, Half-Penny."

At her words, the panic fled the little man's face, being replaced with horrible, despairing acceptance. "Can't Alys. Not that. Not a chance."

"Believe me, Half-Penny, the irony of me making you rat on someone is not lost on me, but I need to find Briar. And I know you know where she is."

Half-Penny Speaks said nothing.

Alys leapt up and crossed over to the man, putting her face inches from his. She was so fast Dax was barely able to follow. Alys grabbed the little man's maimed hand and held it beside their faces. "You owe me," she said, punctuating every word. "You know that me taking your fingers was a kindness. I could have done so much worse."

At her words, Half-Penny went sickly pale and his eyes grew wider than before. A single tear trickled down, leaving a track through the grime on his face. Half-Penny closed his eyes and gave a shuddering gasp before nodding once in a tight, little jerk. Alys released his wrist and Half-Penny stumbled to the chair she had vacated without raising his eyes to look at her.

"Down the street. The old dance house. She holes up there most nights." The filthy little man sounded broken and hollow.

Alys leaned over and patted him on the cheek. "There. That wasn't so hard now, was it?" She looked at Dax. "Looks like you're taking me to the theater, Dax," she said, gesturing toward the door.

Dax turned, anxious to get out of the cramped, foul little residence. He opened the door, grateful for the rush of cold, evening air, but just outside was a figure.

His eyes went to her face and immediately Dax recognized the large, bright eyes. "Laurel?" he said in surprise.

She stared back at him, eyes wide. Her blonde hair was hidden underneath a hood and her mouth was set in a tight grimace. She looked so different than the woman he had met in the palace, but there was no mistaking it was Sergeant Laurel from the Royal Guard.

"Wha—" he managed to get out.

And then she kicked him in the chest.

ACT 7
A LONG TIME COMING

Dax crashed into the table, sending Half-Penny crumpling to the floor underneath him. Already, Alys was in motion, blades flying toward the silhouetted figure. The projectiles flew past as the figure shifted from the doorway and into the darkening street.

Alys darted forward, tucked her head, and leapt through the filthy window, sending shattering glass ringing about her. She rolled to her feet, her scythe, Aunty, off her back and in one hand, and stared across the street into a reflection of herself. Now, seeing with her own eyes, Alys understood how even those who knew her were fooled. The woman was dressed as she was, down to the back-strapped wooden pole. She moved with the same lithe economy of steps that Alys had honed over the years.

The Briarthorn gave Alys a smile and a mocking curtsy. "Ta, Boss," she said. "Or is it Lady Alys now? I haven't been back long enough to catch up on all the gossip."

Alys held Aunty out to the side, the dying light catching the long, curved blade as she began to circle slowly. "I'd say you been around long enough to do plenty, Briar," Alys said. "You wanted my attention? Well, now you got it."

The Briar pursed her lips in a pout and shook her head. "Alys, that was always your biggest problem. You were always so damn arrogant. What makes you think you were whose attention I wanted?" Shifting her hands, the Briarthorn cast something on the ground and small pops filled the air. A bright flash of light flared and thick smoke followed.

Alys wasn't impressed by tired, old tricks. She charged forward, closing the gap quickly as the blade of her scythe sang through the air. But while it sliced smoke, it bit only empty air.

The tap of wood on stone alerted Alys and she dropped down as the Briar vaulted on her wooden staff, aiming a kick where Alys's head had been. The woman missed wide and landed in a crouch, her back to Alys.

Alys extended her left arm, the weighted end of a garrote falling down from her sleeve. She expertly whipped the weapon toward the Briarthorn's neck. As it wrapped around her throat, the Briar slipped in a small, silver blade, cutting the noose cleanly.

The two women stared at each other on the silent street.

From the side, Alys heard a noise. The Briar tilted her head, gesturing with her chin toward the building. From the corner of her eye, Alys saw Donner helping Dax onto the street. Dax was holding his ribs, but his eyes were wide with shock and confusion.

"I want a meeting with Pious," the Briarthorn said.

Alys did not take her eyes from the other woman. "He won't see you," she said.

The Briar raised a finger and waggled it at Alys. "No lies, Alys. As hard as that will be for you, no lies. We both know that is not true. Pious Black will want to speak with me after what I did. After what I took."

"And what is it you want exactly, Briar?"

The Briarthorn looked at her for a moment and then drew herself up tall. "I want back in the game, Alys. And, for that, after what happened that night, I need Pious's blessing."

Folding her arms across her chest, Alys shook her head. "And you think taking out one of his captains is going to ingratiate you to him? Pious and Cin have never been close, but Cin was always an earner."

"The Cinderman was too weak to hold what he had, so I took it from him," the Briarthorn said. "I won't be that weak. I won't lose what he did. All I ask is for my place at the table again. In return, I'll keep his precious bauble safe."

Alys laughed. "You used to be reckless, Briar, but I see being dead has made you just plain crazy. Why do you think Pious would ever bother to bargain with you?

"Because it worked for you, didn't it, Alys?" the Briar asked. "You stole his and you're still in the game." She shrugged. "So I simply did what you did and stole the stakes."

"You're not me," Alys said.

Briar grinned at her. "No, I'm better."

"Big words, Briar. Care to put them to the test?"

"I would cherish the opportunity, Alys, but my business is with Pious Black. You are just my passage to him."

For a moment, Alys said nothing, staring into the Briathorn's eyes before she gave a small nod. "Tomorrow night, at first bell."

"Where?"

"You know where," Alys replied, her patience wearing thin.

The Briar's pretty face slowly pulled back into a grin. "Ah, nostalgia. Of course. And you speak for Pious Black?"

"No one speaks for Pious Black but Pious," Alys said. "But I will get word to him and if he wants to see you, Briar, he'll be there."

The Briarthorn looked at her for a moment and then nodded. "Believe it or not, it actually is good to see you again, Alys. It has been a long time."

"A lifetime," Alys said.

The Briar bowed her head and then turned and walked down the darkening street into the growing evening fog.

Alys watched her go and resisted the urge to put a knife between her shoulder blades.

ACT 8
THE FAMILY BUSINESS

The morning sun had not crested the horizon when Dax entered the palace. Blowing past a few startled guards, he moved through the corridors at a walk just a hair short of a sprint, while his mind whirled.

He didn't know whether Laurel or the Briarthorn was real. If she was a traitor to the crown or Alys. For better or worse, he had kept his mouth shut on the street. Now, the only thing he knew for certain was he had to get to Marek.

He took the stairs to the First Shield's office two at a time, then, ignoring the final guards, he entered the room like a storm. Despite the early hour, Marek was seated at the large, wooden desk dominating the room.

"You're starting to keep Lowside hours, Dax," Marek said with a small smile.

"Your Sergeant Laurel is not what she seems," Dax said, his eyes focused on his brother. "I saw her in Lowside a few hours ago, when she damn near put her boot through my chest."

Marek nodded. "She felt terrible about that," he said quietly.

Dax's blood ran cold as the desperate drive to warn Marek, to inform him of the dangerous Lowside criminal in his inner circle, disappeared. "You know about her? What the hell is going on, Marek?"

Marek nodded his head and the two guards closed the heavy, wooden door behind them, leaving the two brothers alone.

Dax repeated his question, this time his voice more insistent, "What the hell is going on?"

"Laurel is no traitor. Of that, I can assure you," Marek said. "She is loyal to the crown and to our family."

At that, Dax grimaced.

Marek raised a placating hand. "I know you're upset—"

"You're damn right I'm upset," Dax snapped. "I told you I didn't need looking after, but you put that girl into Lowside anyway. Do you have any idea of the danger she is in?"

Marek gave him a long, level stare. "Laurel is not in Lowside for you, brother."

Dax raised an eyebrow. "What?"

"Think, Dax. I didn't just drop the girl off on the Prionside docks yesterday. Laurel was part of Alys's crew years ago." Crossing the room, Marek opened a decanter and poured generous servings of brandy into two crystal goblets. "You'll want a drink. This may be hard to take in all at once."

"Harder than being duped by my own brother?" Dax asked bitterly. "Harder than learning that an agent of the crown is running around Lowside murdering people?"

Stone-faced, Marek offered him one of the goblets. "Yes, actually."

Dax sent the goblet flying across the room with a quick slap. "You stood in these rooms and you lied to me! You and your loyal sergeant lied to me. I want to know why."

42

"Because we had to know we could trust you," Marek said simply.

Marek's cold, logical tone stabbed Dax in the heart. Sorrow and rage warred within and he blew out a frustrated, disgusted breath. "Did I pass?" he asked bitterly. "Am I worthy of your trust?"

"When it comes to her, when it comes to Alys, yes, we had to be sure you wouldn't just give up Laurel on the spot. That you kept quiet proved to us that deep down, you still know there are lines. That your feelings for Alys haven't blurred everything so that she's the only thing you see." Marek sighed. "Listen, Dax. I am sorry. You don't know how sorry I was to have to do this, but what's at stake is bigger than us. Bigger than Laurel's life, even. She knew that and that's why she gambled on you when she revealed herself."

Dax's mind raced back to the events earlier. When he had seen her, he uttered her name. If he had slipped further, her secret would have been revealed and she would have been killed because of it. Her blood would have been on his hands.

Dax opened his mouth to respond, but Marek stopped him. "Wait, brother. You wanted to know the truth. I will tell you all. The Royal Guard is more than just a collection of shiny breastplates and smart formations to dress up a parade ground. We are men and women who have sworn to protect the crown in matters where the crown cannot be seen to act openly. We protect the king and the kingdom from the dangers that most of the world will never know of." Marek took a sip of brandy before setting the glass carefully onto the desk beside him. "Laurel has been one of our operatives in Lowside since she was a child. She spent years working her way into Pious Black's crew. She was even there that night they tried to kill our father." He shook his head. "But after that night, we pulled her out."

Dax's mind reeled as he stared at his brother like he would a stranger. "And you put her back in for me?"

"Yes, but not for the reason you think. I'm sure you've heard by now what the Cinderman lost? What Laurel reclaimed?"

Dax caught the words Marek used. Not stole. Reclaimed. He offered a small shrug. "They've talked about it, but never put forward what it actually is."

"Of course they haven't," Marek replied. "It's an artifact, Dax. Ancient. Perhaps even older than the First Ascended themselves." He paused. "Do you remember what happened to Alys's friend Kay?"

The blood fled from Dax's face. Ashen, he opened his mouth. "It's that bad?"

"Worse," Marek said. "She had a sliver. This is the whole thing."

Dax barely suppressed a shudder. "How? Where the hell did the Cinderman get something like that?"

"The Cinderman didn't get it, Dax. He was just the keeper. It was Pious Black that got it and he took it from the palace vault." Marek downed the rest of his drink. "He took it that night he came into the palace. Killing our father was only one of his objectives that dark night. While he failed in that mission, he succeeded in breaching the vault."

The weight of the memories almost crushed Dax. No matter what, it seemed that terrible night would haunt him all his life.

Marek continued, "That was not the first attempt for Pious. For decades, he's been at war with the crown. He keeps it quiet, all the while growing his power base. Securing his grip on his part of the city. But make no mistake, he is up to something. He's organizing Lowside." Marek crossed his arms. "We want to take his base of power from him. His captains? The artifacts he stole?

All those just fight the symptoms. What we really seek is a chance to cut out the infection at the source. We need to kill Pious Black."

Dax shook his head. "Why not send in a contingent of Royal Guard and go get him. Hell, call in the army even."

"How do you know that isn't exactly what he wants? An overwhelming show of force from Highside, marching into the streets and alleys of Lowside? The oppressors coming with sword and fire? You're justicar of the Second District, Dax. You've gotten a feel for Lowside and its people. Tell me, how would they react to that?"

Dax said nothing.

"Besides," Marek continued, "he would just slip away. Disappear until he was able to rebuild his strength. He is patient and he is cunning. Far more than you can imagine."

"You sound like you're afraid of him."

"Of course I'm afraid of him!" Marek roared before pausing to take a deep breath. "I'm afraid of him, because I understand him. I know what he is capable of. He must have had the plan for that night for years. Just waiting for that last piece of the puzzle to fall into his lap."

Dax's eyes narrowed. "Alys, you mean. Or me?"

"Both," Marek said. "Nobody can get to Pious unless he wants it. We've tried to get people close over the years and they've always failed. Only a few have even made it back to us alive. And Laurel, she's the only one who's ever gotten out and volunteered to go back in. She can get close to Pious, but she'll never get close enough to learn what we need and then kill him once and for all." Marek paused and met Dax's stare. "There's only one person in all of Resa who can do that. Just one person that Pious truly trusts."

"I will not turn on Alys," Dax said, shaking his head before Marek finished speaking.

"I'm not asking you to." Marek's face softened a fraction. "I would never ask you to, Dax. There are those who think Alys is truly his heir. All darkness and ambition, just like him. But I know her. More than that, I know you, brother," he said, putting a hand on Dax's shoulder. "And I know how much you believe in her."

Marek paused and Dax saw hesitation before his brother continued, "I know what happened that night, Dax. Everything. How father warned you that she had lied to you. How he warned you that she was an assassin sent from Pious Black to kill him. How you tried desperately to convince father he was wrong about her."

"Stop," said Dax quietly.

"And how crushed you were when Alys came out from the shadows, her blade red with the blood of the Royal Guard."

"Enough, Marek! Please, stop."

"No. Listen, brother. I don't say this to hurt you. I said I know what happened that night, Dax. I know it all. When father fell, he was not unconscious. He heard the rest of what happened. How you stood up to her." He looked at Dax. "I know she made you choose between her and our father's life. And you chose to save our father."

The memories encased Dax, suffocating him. Everything he hoped to move past, to bury or resolve, came down upon his head. He collapsed into one of the chairs.

Marek knelt beside him. "Listen to me," he said, his voice strong, cutting through Dax's pain. "That moment reaffirmed father's faith in you and his hatred for Alys, but I asked myself one question that father, blinded by his hatred of her, could not ask." He looked at Dax. "Could she have beaten you?"

"What do you mean?"

"You've seen Alys fight. Even those years back, there is no way you could have truly stopped her if she was intent on completing her mission. She could have overpowered you and finished father

46

off, but she didn't, Dax. Don't you see? In that moment, you chose our father, but Alys chose you."

Dax's eyes grew wet. "Don't you think I know that? I relive the events of that cursed night every time I close my eyes, Marek! It haunts me!"

"Then help me make things right again," Marek demanded.

Dax shook his head. "What are you saying?"

"I didn't know how much you truly meant to her until I heard that story." His brother took him by the shoulders. "It wasn't Alys that was the true threat, Dax. It was, and is, Pious Black." He paused for a moment and then sat back on his heels. "We need Alys to get to Pious Black..."

"And you need me to get to Alys."

Marek nodded. "But we only want Pious," he said. "She'll be free, truly free, Dax. Once we get him. You have my word on it. More than that, you have the word of the king himself."

"The king knows?"

"Of course he does. This is no game, Dax. This is the safety of the crown and the kingdom. It is a duty I have sworn my life to. It is a duty that Laurel has shown she is willing to sacrifice her life and even her very identity for."

Marek stood in front of Dax. "So now, brother, you know the whole truth. If you reveal what you know to Alys, it will mean a lot of good people will bleed for it, including Laurel. The question is what will you do?"

Dax stared blankly ahead, all rage and energy gone. He slumped over and buried his head in his hands. Marek sat beside him and the two watched through the window as the morning sun rose over the shining spires of the capital.

Act 9
Our Choices Define Us

Alys tightened the buckles binding her jacket. The beaded braids in her hair had been pulled back and tied close to her scalp. She twisted quickly, but there was no rattle or stray noise anywhere about her person. Satisfied, Alys turned to the long table where she had laid out her armory and began selecting what would best accessorize her evening ensemble.

At the end of the table was Dax. In the flickering light of the candles, Alys saw his pensive scowl reflected in the gleaming metal blades spread out on the dark wood. He had been quiet tonight and it seemed there was an unusual intensity to his brooding.

"Out with it, already. What is it you want to say?"

"Don't go to this meeting," Dax muttered.

There was something in his tone that caused her to pause, but she put on a broad, confident smile and winked. "You're sweet, Dax, always have been, but you should know better than to worry about little old me by now." She picked up another blade and made the dagger dance about her knuckles and fingers. "Believe me, I can handle Briar just fine."

"It's not her I'm worried about," he said. "It's Pious Black."

Alys smiled. "If that's what's got you frowning so hard, then have no fear. I can handle Pious Black as well."

"Pious Black is the most wanted man in the kingdom, Alys. The worst kind of person this city breeds." He shook his head. "I don't know why you can't see that."

"I have seen more from Pious Black than you can imagine, dear Dax. And do not for a moment think that I am blind to what he is. The evil and cruelty that he is not only capable of, but that is a part of who he is." She shook her head. "But he has to be that way. That's what you've never understood, no matter how much time you spend down here. Pious Black is order, Dax. He keeps things running. He keeps everything in their place."

Dax crossed his arms. "And that is why you respect him? Because you know your place? Happily beneath him?"

"I respect him, because I believe what he believes," Alys shot back. "Everything does have a place and order is better than blood on the streets. I know it's hard for you to believe, Justicar, but it is not the king's justice that keeps a person safe in Lowside. It is the universal fear of Pious Black.

"People pay for protection. They get protected. Gangs and crews have their territories and they stay where they're supposed to be. Where they belong. Conflict is confined, people are safe, and everything runs like it's supposed to." She turned away in exasperation. "The only time there's a problem is when people try to cross where they don't belong. You and I should know that better than anyone."

Dax rose to his feet. "I hate it when you talk like that."

"What? The truth? I thought we promised to stop telling each other pretty lies a long time ago."

"I never lied to you," he said emphatically, the conviction in his voice raw and powerful. "I was always true about how I felt for you. I was the one who got used, remember? Pious used you to try and kill my father."

Alys rounded on him, her eyes flaring. "I don't know what's sadder," she snapped. "That you think Pious put me up to anything or that you still feel no responsibility for what happened."

"I do," he said, pain obvious on his face. "I play that night over and over in my mind, Alys, and I regret it every moment of my days." He took a deep, shuddering breath and lowered his head. "For years, I tried to forgive you, but I could not even do that, because there was nothing to forgive. I know that now. It was my failure that night, Alys. Mine." He took her hands into his own.

His skin felt warm on hers and, for a brief moment, she could not let go. Alys stared into his eyes and saw something different: a feverish light. He meant every word. He was different now.

And a dark whisper in the back of her mind hissed the reason why.

Dax had learned something.

Alys tightened her grip. "Who have you been talking to?"

"What? Talking to?"

"I know you, Dax. Something's changed."

Confusion gave way to pain and exasperation as Dax shook off her touch. "Absolutely typical," he said through gritted teeth. "I am pouring my heart out—"

"Right, because that hasn't ever gotten us into trouble before." She dipped her head, trying to catch his eyes again. "Why now, Dax? You've been back in Lowside for months. Why is this coming out tonight?"

Shaking his head, Dax returned to his chair. He looked drained, desperate. "I just—" he started before swallowing hard. "I just want to start over," he said, looking back up at her. "Let's get out of here, Alys. Out of Resa. Far, far away from everything. Like we promised each other at the very beginning. Back before there was a Pious Black—"

"Or a High Chancellor Ellis?"

"Yes!" Dax said, slapping a hand on the table. "Yes. Back before it all went to hell."

Alys studied his eyes. The honest, open, trusting eyes of the good man she had first fallen in love with a lifetime ago. But those eyes were so trusting because they were ultimately blind.

No, she could not leave Resa and she could never leave with Dax. She knew that for a truth, no matter how his eyes tried to weaken her.

The old man had been right. Dax made her weak.

"I'm sorry, Dax," she whispered. "It can't be. We can't be. Not while your father lives."

"But why?" Dax asked.

"Because your father is a monster," Alys said. "You don't know the things he's done."

He shot to his feet. "Then tell me!" he demanded. "You never told me that night. You just made me choose while you held a blade to my father's throat, the corpses of good, honest men in your wake!"

In her mind, Alys remembered the faces of those good, honest men. Members of Ellis's Royal Guard who had dragged her from home years earlier. Who had laughed while she screamed and begged the Chancellor for her life. The feeling of shame and helplessness came rushing back. Feelings long dead.

Through gritted teeth, Alys spoke, "There are things I will never tell you, Dax. That I can never tell you."

"Why?"

She looked him fully in the face. "Because I can't trust you."

In that moment, she saw the words cut him as deeply as any knife. His face fell and the devastation hurt her heart even to see it.

"I—I can..." Dax stammered, his words trailing off into helpless, empty breath. "Give me the chance to win that trust back."

Alys saw how much pain he was in. Best to finish it quick. "Talk is cheap, Justicar. You showed your true colors that night. I can't trust you. Not anymore. Not ever again. What you're talking about can never be, no matter how much you may want it," she finished, the last words choked with emotion. She crossed to the table and picked up a viciously curved knife. "And besides, you should know by now," she said, her voice as cold and carefree as the edged steel, "there are no second chances in Lowside."

A long silence filled the room before Dax stood, slowly pushing away from the table. He picked her scythe off the table and offered Alys its long handle. "Then I suppose it's a good thing I come from Highside," he said. "I may never regain your trust, but it won't ever stop me from trying."

His words caught her flatfooted. For the first time, Alys couldn't think of anything clever to say. Her hand closed around the handle of the scythe.

Dax turned away while belting on his sword. "I'm going with you," he said decisively. "I will not get in your way and I do not intend anything reckless or stupid. I am no justicar tonight," he said, pointing to his gray, striped coat hanging by the door.

"Dax—"

"You keep saying I am lacking in my Lowside education. What better way to learn than by meeting the master himself tonight? The mysterious Pious Black." He shrugged. "You were right about this being the wrong night for this. You're right about a lot of things, but not all. Either way, I'm going with you tonight.

Besides, someone has to keep you safe. I think the Briarthorn may be faster than you."

She wanted to argue, to tell him he wasn't coming, but instead she only smirked. "Oh, Daxton, you're adorable when you try and lie."

"It is the curse of the good man," he said, putting a hand mockingly over his heart.

That was the truth, Alys thought. The curse of the best man she had ever, or would ever, know.

Alys pulled up the hood of her cloak. "Let's not keep Briar and Pious waiting."

ACT 10
BLOOD AND BONE

Night was the time Lowside was most active, but tonight, as Dax followed Alys and Donner through dimly lit streets and alleys, there was hardly anyone out. The quiet, empty streets were filled with thick fog, harboring strange, breathless anticipation.

He found it unsettling.

"Quiet out," Dax said.

"It's because Pious Black is out on the streets tonight," the old man said. "And all of Lowside knows it."

Dax smirked. "I thought he cared more for secrecy than that."

"It's not about secrets, boy. It's about fear. The rabbits always know when the wolf is about."

"If you two are done chatting, perhaps you could focus on the task at hand," Alys said.

The rest of the walk was silent. Dax's familiarity with Lowside and its particular areas had grown since he had become justicar. They were nearing the border of Prionside, where the Prion River cut through the city like a mud-colored scar, and where Blacktide Harry held sway as one of Pious Black's chief captains.

Before they headed into the river district though, Alys led them along a long, broad avenue, lined with large warehouses. She stopped before one that looked long since abandoned.

Alys put her hands on her hips. "Might as well come on out, Briar," she said, her words drifting into the thick fog.

From the direction opposite the way they had come, the Briarthorn strolled toward them from the mist. Her hood was back and her wide, bright eyes seemed to catch the moonlight. She carried herself so differently now than she had in Marek's palace office that it was difficult to believe both versions were the same person.

"I'm here, right on time," the Briarthorn said. "I remember how much you value punctuality, Alys."

"It's one of the few things that elevates us above the animals, Briar," Alys responded with a sweet smile.

Briar turned and regarded the large warehouse before them. "Hasn't changed much since we used to meet here to plan jobs. Though not in the best of repair, if I'm going to be totally honest."

Alys shrugged. "Not much call for it these days. Been a while since I ran a crew. Work alone now."

Briar grinned before pointedly looking at Dax. "I can see how... alone you are, Alys." Her eyes scoured Dax like she was assessing him for the auction block.

Dax resisted the urge to shift under the scrutiny, instead fixing her with a hard stare.

Gesturing to Dax, Alys smiled broadly. "Highside here is just along to watch the fun. You explaining to Pious Black why you went after one of his captains and stole one of his most prized possessions should be an enlightening experience for him."

Briar's face grew serious. "It worked when you did it, Alys. When you stole one to secure your freedom and your place at the table. That's all I'm asking Pious for."

Alys lowered herself into a deep bow. "Then after you, Briar. Time to meet the man himself."

The Briarthorn turned and walked to the warehouse's wooden door. As her hand rested upon the handle, Dax fought an urge to call out and warn her. This was the Briarthorn, not Sergeant Laurel.

The door opened and Briar stepped into the dark building, with Alys right behind. Dax held his breath and followed.

In the center of the cavernous space, a solitary figure sat upon a towering pyramid of stacked crates. Small lanterns cast light that both revealed and obscured the elevated man. He was long and lanky, his legs drawn up as he sat upon the makeshift throne. His right hand rested on a long-handled axe, its vicious-looking head catching the flickering lantern light. He looked up and Dax saw a long scar that cut across his left eye, the orb itself cold and dull white, like a full moon. That dead eye seemed to take them all in. Measuring them.

This was the infamous Pious Black, absolute ruler of Lowside. Just being in his presence, Dax could understand why.

Pious Black drummed his fingers against the axe, filling the room with sound. "You have something of mine," he said in a cold, almost disinterested voice.

The Briarthorn gave a small shrug and Dax could not help but admire the woman's courage. "The Cinderman was careless with it," she said. "I picked it up for safekeeping."

"How fortunate for me that you were such a kind, responsible soul and not an opportunistic little thief I should leave choking on her own blood," Pious Black said.

At his words, dark-clad figures stepped from the warehouse's shadowed recesses.

The Briarthorn looked around. "Fortunate indeed," she said, maintaining her calm. "But I will tell you what else I am most definitely not and that is stupid. Should anything happen to me tonight, your precious bauble would have to find its way to someone else."

"And who might that be, Briarthorn?"

Briar pointed at Dax. "Why, his father, of course."

Dax almost swallowed his own tongue before a long moment of Razor-edged silence.

Suddenly, Pious Black threw back his head and laughed. It was an ugly, cruel sound. "This one has some sand, I'll say that for her. What do you make of her, Alys? Is she all flower or are there thorns on this Briar?"

"She can prick," Alys said. "Though she's not nearly the edge she imagines herself to be."

Pious spun the axe around on its handle. "Neither were you, once upon a day, girl." He settled back, his eyes focused on Briar, as if weighing her future.

Then the door exploded.

The force threw Dax to the ground as the room was bathed in fire, heat stealing the breath from his lungs. He scrambled forward, trying to regain his footing while thick, black smoke filled the building.

Squinting, Dax saw figures wearing heavy, black aprons and masks with small, opaque goggles. They carried wicked-looking blades and cudgels while pouring through the wall of flame where the door used to be. All around was chaos.

One of the men turned his strange, insect-like protective mask toward Dax. With a muffled roar, the man charged, raising a large butcher's cleaver high above his head. With little time, Dax reached for the dirk concealed in his boot. Just as he drew the blade, the man was blasted off his feet.

Through watering eyes, Dax saw Alys finish the man. She was wearing one of the strange, hooded masks his attacker had been sporting. There was a bright splash of blood across its base that Dax knew was not from her.

Alys ripped the now-dead man's mask off and tossed it to Dax. "Put it on!" she ordered.

Dax slipped the thing over his head. It stunk like sweat and blood, but kept stinging smoke from his eyes. "What the hell is going on?" he shouted over roaring flames and wild fighting.

"It's the Cinderman," Alys said. "Bastard didn't want to wait for Pious to come for his head, so he's taking his shot."

A wild, charging man in a black apron came at them, but Dax had his sword drawn and stabbed the man. The man shuddered and collapsed to the ground. Dax had to hold the hilt of his blade tight to keep it from being wrenched from his hand. "This is no shot!" he shouted at Alys. "This is a damn war!"

"You have to hand it to old Cinderman, he really is putting his all into this," Dax heard from nearby as Donner emerged from the smoke, a large, wooden cudgel resting on his shoulder.

Everywhere, people rushed and fought. Dax had lost sight of Laurel in the chaos. Briarthorn, he corrected himself. Both she and Pious Black had been lost in the tumble of crates during the initial gout of flame.

"There's at least thirty leather-aprons dusting it up in here with Pious's boys and we're caught right in the middle," Alys said as she stepped forward, swinging her scythe in a wide arc, forcing away a menacing group of masked and aproned fighters.

Through the smoke, Dax caught sight of Pious Black standing in the center of the warehouse on one of the overturned boxes, smashing his long-handled axe into man after man. His own face was bare and soot and ash mixed with the blood of enemies to create a fearsome mask. He laughed like a madman as he murdered all who dared approach.

More shocking than that was the Briarthorn at his back, fighting savagely to protect him. She had two long knives cutting and stabbing with ruthless efficiency.

Alys charged forward. She held the scythe in front of her, forcing combatants out of the way until she stood before Pious. "Time to go," she said.

Over the roaring chaos, Dax heard a voice screaming out orders. "There he is! There he is! Kill him! Kill him now!" The words repeated across the warehouse and Dax caught a fleeting glimpse of the Cinderman's shrieking form.

A wave of Cinderman's masked thugs rushed forward. Dax had his sword in one hand and his dagger in the other. As the mass of fighting men hit, he put both to use. There was no place for technique or footwork while he cut and smashed and kicked at anything that came near.

A gloved hand reached toward his mask. Dax smashed his head forward, catching the man in the nose and sending him down to the ground.

Alys pointed toward the rear of the warehouse. "Look!" The flames had eaten through the wall and smoke billowed into the Lowside night. "Go!" she yelled.

Pious Black spun his axe before leaping from the crate and running for the opening. Briar was at his heels, and then Alys, Dax, and Donner. They darted through the opening just as the flames collapsed the wall behind them.

Donner scanned the alley for any of Cinderman's fighters and saw Pious Black near the Briarthorn.

"You wanted a place at the table?" Pious Black said to her. "Tonight, you earned it. At least until I change my mind and kill you."

Briar was breathing hard, soot staining her sweaty face. "And your property?"

"I'll tell you when I want it," Pious Black said before hefting his axe onto his shoulder. "Alys," he called out.

Alys hefted her scythe. "This one's double the usual rate," she said.

Pious Black smiled his cruel, bloody lips. "You should be paying me, girl. I know how much it thrills you when you get to put down one of my captains."

"Double, Pious."

"Fine," he responded, as if the number was inconsequential. "Double for the head of the Cinderman." He raised a finger. "But I want his last moments to allow him time to contemplate his ill-advised coup." He smiled. "And I would like to see his remorse on his face when you bring me his head."

Dax wanted to pull Alys close and tell her no, but it was clear she had already made her decision.

Her eyes met his for a moment before she looked to Donner. "Get Dax back to the Second District Precinct House, old man. The last thing we need is a justicar dying in Lowside tonight." Slipping her scythe onto her back, Alys scrambled up the side of the adjoining building. She moved quick and effortlessly, melting into the shadows as soon as she slipped over the side of the roof.

When Dax looked back down, Pious Black was gone.

For one brief moment, Briar caught Dax's eye, and he saw something. A glimpse of the woman he had first met in the palace. Then it was gone, replaced by the Briarthorn's hard, green eyes. She gave a small bow. "All in all, a successful night for me, boys.

Walk home careful now. Streets aren't safe this time of night." She turned and ran down the alley.

"Come along, boy. I'll get you back to your office," Donner said.

ACT 11
FOR KING AND COUNTRY

Dax slumped into the chair behind the desk. His dark clothes reeked of smoke, the smell of it filling his small office. Aching pain from sore muscles and minor wounds made his body a symphony of misery.

None was as bad as the pain in his heart.

In his mind, Dax replayed Alys disappearing over the edge of the roof, heading to murder a man at the behest of Pious Black. She would never be free while Pious Black ran Lowside.

"Welcome to the fight, Lord Ellis," a soft voice came from behind.

Startled, Dax leapt to his feet, reaching for the dagger at his belt. By the window, a shadow detached from the darkness and the Briarthorn stepped into the light cast from the candle on Dax's desk.

Composing himself, Dax crossed his arms. "You seem confident of my loyalty now," he said, an edge of bitterness to his voice.

"I never doubted you for a moment, Lord. That is why I made sure to present myself to you in the palace."

Dax moved back to his chair, too tired to remain standing. "Dax," he said. "Please, just Dax."

"Fair enough."

She seemed an odd mixture of formal palace guard and smirking Lowside killer. Laurel and Briarthorn both. It occurred to Dax that perhaps, in this office, between her two worlds, this might be her truest version. He dismissed that thought almost immediately as Alys's chiding voice echoed in his head, warning him truth was something only afforded when you came from Highside.

Uncomfortable in the silence, Dax spoke, "My brother said you have been undercover in Lowside since you were a child. How is that even possible?"

Laurel seated herself on the edge of his desk. "I was born in Lowside."

"If you were born here, why help Highside?"

She gave him a small smile. "The standard answer is that I'm not helping Highside. I'm protecting the crown and the people of the Kingdom of Aedaron," she said. Her smile faded a touch. "But if you were born here, raised here, like me, you'd understand that it is more than that." She looked him in the eyes, her large, blue eyes open and honest. "The slums aren't romantic. Lowside is the darkness and it will swallow up everything, if we let it. Highside is the light. Captain Marek gave me an opportunity to join the light and keep the darkness at bay. How could I not accept?"

Dax drew a deep breath. "I am sorry about what I said to you the other day, in the palace. I questioned your skill and your conviction."

"There is no need for apology, sir. I expected it. She's quite charismatic and a gifted deceiver. And the two of you have quite a shared history."

Dax stiffened. "Given the dual life you've led for the last decade, I don't know that you get to cast judgement on anyone's honesty."

"I am sorry if I offended you, sir. I shroud myself in lies," she agreed, "but I lie for a cause. For something I believe in and want to protect." She stared out the window, looking on the streets of Lowside. "But I have known Alys a long time and I can tell you she lies because it is her nature. And that's what makes her so dangerous. She doesn't deceive on purpose. She just can't help it. It is who she is, down to her very core. Her heart is dark."

Dax looked away. "I don't believe that. I can't."

For a long moment, they sat in the dark room, the single candle flickering.

"So, how's this going to work now, Laurel?" Dax asked.

"It's Briarthorn," she corrected, "or Briar, but never Laurel."

He nodded.

"As Briarthorn, I will stay close to Alys, stay active in Lowside, and follow whatever instructions I receive from your brother. But above all, I will look out for opportunities."

"Opportunities?" Dax asked. "Opportunities for what?"

"For the only thing that ultimately matters," Briar said. "To kill Pious Black."

Dax furrowed his brow. "You had the perfect opportunity tonight," he said. "In the fight, in the warehouse. You had dozens of chances to kill him there. Why didn't you strike then?"

"Because Pious Black is smart, sir. Because Pious Black is dangerous and a master of deception." Her blue eyes sparkled in the candlelight. "I've never met him, but I know this. That man in the warehouse was not Pious Black."

ACT 12
BEST SERVED COLD

The interior of the small curio shop was quiet as Alys poured herself a drink. She ignored the dried blood on the back of her hand as the liquor swished around the battered, tin cup, knowing it would wash away. It always did.

"I take it the Cinderman was surprised to see you," the old man said, comfortably seated behind his counter.

Alys put her drink down. "Can you drop the act now, please?"

The old man smiled at her in a false apology. "But Donner is always one of my favorite parts to play, girl." He laughed, but as he did, his voice and posture shifted and changed until Donner was gone.

And in his place was Pious Black.

"So, Cinderman?" Pious asked pointedly.

Alys drained her drink in one quick belt and poured herself another. She threw him a bloody sack.

Pious looked inside and smiled. "Oh, his expression is perfect. Surprised indeed. Well done. It will go nicely with his wife and children. I'm thinking we should display them all at the Night Circus. No point wasting them at the Foundry. Everyone there already knows the score."

Alys shrugged. "That's your business, Pious. You paid for the Cinderman's head. You've got it. Anything after that, I'm not interested."

"Oh, Alys. When did you get so damn serious about everything," he said with a crooked smile. Pious took the bottle from Alys and poured himself a drink. "Ellis and his Royal Guard are up to something again. They're making a move. And even money that boy's involved."

For a moment, fear flared within her. "Dax would not turn on me," Alys said, her voice calm.

"If it comes girl... when it comes," he amended. "He might not even realize he is turning on you. Ellis can use so much to twist his mind." He picked up his drink and swirled the remainder around the glass.

"Don't worry. I have him under control."

"Do you?"

"Since when have you doubted me?"

"Since the last time the boy was the reason you failed me." He fixed her with cold eyes. "I've gotten older and my senses aren't what they once were, but it's clear as day that boy's still got a hold on you. Have you forgotten what his father did to you?"

"That he sent men to take me from my home? That he stabbed me over and over and then left me to die bleeding out into the streets?"

"Exactly that." Pious Black's eyes had a faraway look, like he was remembering something form long ago. "But you didn't die, girl. You came back stronger."

"Because of you. I haven't forgotten."

Pious Black raised his glass in a salute.

"I came back to settle the score and I will do just that." Alys rolled the empty cup in her hand and then set it carefully on the counter.

"Good, because I believe it's finally time to make our move and your boy is just the way to do it. He trusts you. We can use him." He paused for a moment. His eyes bore into her, all trace of humor gone. "That is, unless you're still that lovestruck little girl."

For a moment, all Alys could think of was Dax. His earnest pleading with her earlier in the evening. His desperate hope to run and start over. For them each to be free. But she killed those thoughts.

She could show no weakness. No sliver of doubt. Not unless she wanted to end up like the Cinderman.

Or worse. To have Dax end up that way.

No. The two of them had had their chance at happiness. Now, it was gone.

There were no second chances in Lowside.

She looked directly into the dark eyes of Pious Black, inviting his piercing gaze, daring his scrutiny and judgement. And smiled.

"Try me, old man."

Pious Black grinned.

ACKNOWLEDGMENTS

Mark: To my brother Dave, my wife Tiffany, and my son Bryce for their love and support. And to my mom and dad, Dan and Pam Gelineau, who I miss every day, and who made me everything I am.

Joe: To Irene, Emma, and Kate. Because of you, I know I can do, and be, anything. In every way that counts, these stories are for you.

A very special thanks to Jason. His beautiful work on our website, ebooks, and paperbacks has been inspiring, and his dogged editing and persistence has pushed us to become better on every level. But most of all, he believed in us, often times more than we believed in ourselves, and that is something that we will never forget or ever fully repay.

And a huge thank you to the rest of our insanely talented (and far too good for the likes of us) team.

Our copy editor, TJ Redig, whose humor and skill keeps both us and our stories moving. And of course to Marija at Damonza, our cover designer, who blows us away every time she brings our characters and world to life.

Finally, to our supremely patient and forgiving beta readers: Emily, Maria, and Patrick. Thank you, thank you, and thank you. We ask a lot of you, and we ask it a lot! But you are always there for us. We wouldn't be here without you.

AUTHOR'S NOTE
ECHOES OF THE ASCENDED, BOOKS 2

We thought we knew what we were getting into.

We did not.

We were fools.

But after finishing this second round of books, we are grateful that we were and still remain foolish enough to keep our heads down and just keep moving forward.

It was a difficult year. Mark lost his father, after losing his mother only a year before. In many ways, it was because of Mark's mother that we even took these tentative first steps, and this past year, it was his father that inspired us every day to keep going.

He was a great man.

Thinking about our own families and all things said and unsaid, we both realized how much of our hearts are in our stories.

Our characters are brave and foolish and believe in things that perhaps they shouldn't. So did our parents. And one day, that is our hope for our children as well.

It's cheezy, it's sappy, but having kids will do that to you!

But that's us. Writers. Fathers. Fools.

Thank you for taking a chance on us and our stories and for coming along for the ride.

We'll see you again for books 3, out in a few months. Til then, we hope you too are foolish enough to keep chasing the things you love.

Mark & Joe

GELINEAU AND KING

Thank you for reading this Gelineau and King novella.

Visit us on the web at www.gelineauandking.com and join us on our mailing list for the latest releases, news, and promotions.

Like us at facebook.com/gelineauandking.

Follow us on Twitter @gelineauandking.

Or send us your best wishes via astral projection. Whatever your medium, we accept love in all its forms. Hope to see you again soon.

PREVIEW

FAITH AND MOONLIGHT
PART 2

ROAN

Roan huddled in the wooden cage.

Evening was giving way to night and the air was growing colder. His breath streamed into the dying light, drifting between the bars of the cage.

Over by the fire, men drank and laughed while the smell of food made his mouth water. He tore his eyes away and looked to another cage. Inside it, a boy waited, his eyes locked on the men and their meal. The boy looked older than Roan's seven summers and taller by almost a hand width.

It didn't matter.

It was almost time.

Roan clenched and unclenched his fists as he crouched behind the cage door.

The Dogwatcher approached, his leathery face stained with grease and ale. "Hungry, pup?" the Dogwatcher asked. "Then you know what to do," he said, kicking open the cage door.

Roan darted for the other boy and the two of them met in a vicious tackle in the center of the clearing. At the impact, the men around the fire cheered.

Roan slipped out of the hold, wrapping an arm around the bigger boy's neck as he moved behind him. The boy dropped to his back, smashing down upon Roan and driving air from his lungs. Roan tried to hold on, but the boy broke free, turning and throwing wild punches.

A punch landed squarely in his nose and Roan's world went white. Blood spurted as the boy kept punching.

Roan desperately reached with his free hand and felt the smooth weight of stone in the cold earth. Grabbing the rock, he swung it into the boy's head, knocking him sprawling backwards. Roan jumped on top and struck him again in the head. The rock came away wet with blood.

The boy cried and flailed as Roan struck again and again.

Finally, the boy's arms fell limp. The rock was warm and wet in Roan's hand and everything was stained with blood. Breathing hard, Roan looked to the Dogwatcher.

The man spat into the fire and gave a half-nod.

Roan gripped the rock in both hands and raised it high.

***

Roan awoke. His blankets were gone and his nightclothes were covered in sweat.

The bandit camp was gone. The cage was gone. He was back in the school dormitory. The other boys slept soundlessly in their beds.

Blood roared in his head, a slowly fading tumult from the nightmare.

No, not a nightmare.

A memory of the boy he'd killed.

The boy whose name he'd never know.

Roan shook the feeling off. Good, he thought. Good.

He had to remember what he was, who he had been before Kay and the others had taken him in. And he had to remember why he was still here.

Kay.

Here, she could have a new life of promise and joy and belonging. A life she deserved.

A life he owed her.

If he had to fight others and face his past, so be it.

For Kay, what wouldn't he endure?

Kay

Kay awoke in terror.

She found herself standing in a grass field on the far side of school. Her nightclothes were soaked with dew and the edges of their fabric were ragged and torn. There were leaves in her hair and the knuckles on both her hands were raw and bloody.

Just like the week before.

These dreams were coming more frequently now.

Worst of all, within her heart was a low, dull ache in the place she had forced the sliver of Behayer's blade. The sliver Gideon had given her. It began there, but radiated to her fingers and toes and behind her eyes.

Doubling over, she rolled into a fetal position on the wet grass. She bit her lips to keep from crying out as her chest burned in agony, scared she would alert the groundskeepers or guards.

It had seemed so simple. Roan would never have stayed if she failed. When Gideon offered her the means to secure Roan's admission into Faith, she took it. She knew there would be a cost.

But this? This?

As the first fingers of dawn crept over the tall marble towers of the school of Faith, Kay finally sat up, held her knees to her chest and sobbed quietly alone.

She didn't know what was happening to her, but she did know it was just beginning.

Best Left in the Shadows

A Highside girl. Beaten. Murdered. Her body found on a Lowside dock. A magistrate comes looking for answers. For justice.

Alys trades and sells secrets among the gangs and factions of Lowside. She is a daughter of the underworld. Bold. Cunning. Free. When an old lover asks for help, she agrees. For a price.

Together, they travel into the dark heart of the underworld in search of a killer.

"I was blown away by the detail and world building that was accomplished in so few pages. I didn't feel like I was seeing a section of a puzzle, more like I was reading a story that would contribute to a larger whole, but is compelling and rich all on its own."

– Mama Reads, Hazel Sleeps

CIVIL BLOOD
BEST LEFT IN THE SHADOWS BOOK 2

One city. Two worlds.

Alys and Dax have always been caught in the middle. Once they fought for love, and their worlds tore them apart. But now as they are forced back together, they must choose whether to fight once again.

But for what? And against whom? In the world of Lowside, nothing is as it seems.

Even each other.

"[A] lightning quick story of criminal confrontations, old feelings, and rousing fights... Gelineau and King have so much more to reveal before this mesmerizing tale is done."

– Bookwraiths

A Reaper of Stone

A Lady is dead. Her noble line ended. And the King's Reaper has come to reclaim her land and her home. In the marches of Aedaron, only one thing is for certain. All keeps of the old world must fall.

Elinor struggles to find her place in the new world. She once dreamed of great things. Of becoming a hero in the ways of the old world. But now she is a Reaper. And her duty is clear. Destroy the old. Herald the new.

"A classic fantasy tale with a strong, admirable heroine and a nice emotional punch. Great start to an enjoyable new series!"

    – RL King, author of *The Alastair Stone Chronicles*

Broken Banners
A Reaper of Stone book 2

Slaughtered and left for crows, soldiers of the King's Army lay dead in a field. A grim reminder: the king's law ends at the gates of the capital.

Elinor fought for what she believed and now she is an outcast. No soldier will follow her. No officer will stand with her. Yet when she finds her brothers and sisters slaughtered, she cannot turn her back on them.

Long ago, they swore an oath. Not to the king, but to each other.

And woe to those who break that bond.

"[A] short epic, full of hope and victory where none can be found... The world these authors created is unbelievably tangible."

– Twin Reads

Rend the Dark

The great Ruins are gone. The titans. The behemoths. All banished to the Dark and nearly forgotten. But the cunning ones, the patient ones remain. They hide not in the cracks of the earth or in the shadows of the world. But inside us. Wearing our skin. Waiting. Watching.

Once haunted by visions of the world beyond, Ferran now wields that power to hunt the very monsters that he once feared. He is not alone. Others bear the same terrible burden. But Hunter or hunted, it makes no difference. Eventually, everything returns to the Dark.

"Atmospheric, fast paced, engaging quick read, with a satisfying story and glimpses of Supernatural *and King's* IT.*"*

– *BooksChatter*

Skinshaper
Rend the Dark book 2

Barricades broken.

A mining town empty.

One survivor swings in a cage, waiting to die.

Ferran's tattoos burn as horrors near. They should run. They should seek help. But to save a few, they must journey deeper into the heart of the nightmare to face an ancient foe.

"Skinshaper *will haunt your thoughts long after you have finished reading it, and yet it will leave you wanting more.*"

– Dee is Reading

FAITH AND MOONLIGHT PART 1

Roan and Kay are orphans. A fire destroys their old life, but they have one chance to enter the School of Faith.

They are given one month to pass the entry trials, but as Roan excels and Kay fails, their devotion to each other is put to the test.

They swore they would face everything together, but when the stakes are losing the life they've always dreamed of, what will they do to stay together?

What won't they do?

"You can really feel Roan's desire and dream to be something more and you can also feel Kay's frustration and struggle. And underneath all that you can practically touch how much they care about each other."

– *White Sky Project*